D1344281

Aberdeenshire Library and Information Service
www.aberdeenshire.gov.uk/libraries
Renewals Hotline 01224 661511

26 FEB 2009

12 JAN 2010

22. JAN 20.

1 8 APR 2011

- 1 JUN 2011

- 8 MAR 2012

1 6 OCT 2015

1 5 NOV 2016

0 6 DEC 2016

10. APR 17.

26. APR 17.

16. NOV 17.

28. JUN 18.

Francome, John

Winner takes
all / John
Francome

LP

1712062

WINNER TAKES ALL

John Francome

BBC
LARGE
PRINT

First published in 2006 by
Headline Book Publishing
This Large Print edition published
2006 by BBC Audiobooks by
arrangement with
Headline Book Publishing

ISBN 10: 1 4056 2204 0
ISI Francome, John   204 2

      Winner takes all
Copyri / John Francome   rancome

            LP

        1712062
The ri... ....ome and
Mike Bailey to be identified as the
authors of the work has been
asserted by them in accordance with
the Copyright, Designs and Patents
Act 1988.

British Library Cataloguing in Publication Data available

Printed and bound by CPI Antony Rowe, Eastbourne

CHAPTER ONE

'Here they come now.'

Ben Sayers pointed into the early-morning mist swirling across the broad green gallops above the Berkshire village of Lambourn. He was up here almost every day of the year, working with the thirty-odd racehorses that he trained, putting them through their paces. Sometimes, the people who owned the horses kept him company and he'd tell them of their animal's progress. On these occasions, more often than not, he would have to stretch the truth a little. All racehorse owners were dreamers at heart and it wasn't his job to destroy their hopes. The reality of race day would do that soon enough.

But there was no need for him to lie to the woman standing by his side. The last time Christina Marcus had watched her horse Smokescreen on the gallops the animal could hardly keep himself warm. But today he was back on form. She only had to stand and watch.

A small group of horses burst out of the mist in a thunder of hoofbeats and a jingle of tack. At their head was a big powerful chestnut with a white blaze across his face. The lad in the saddle fought to hold him back but Smokescreen was enjoying himself. He lengthened his stride, leaving his companions trailing. As the horse streaked past, the ground seemed to tremble beneath their feet.

Christina gasped, her full pink lips shaped in wonder as she turned to Ben. There was joy and disbelief in her face. 'You're a miracle-worker,' she exclaimed and threw her arms around him.

Awkwardly, Ben broke free of her grip. He had no objection to being hugged by a pretty woman but not this one. Getting too friendly with the ex-wife of his most important owner was not sensible. That was putting it mildly. Alan Marcus had sixteen horses in training with Ben, almost half of the animals in his yard. He could buy Ben's business with the loose change in his pocket. And he was not the forgiving sort—he'd not forgiven Christina for walking out on their marriage, for a start.

If Ben were honest, getting Smokescreen fit to race again was probably not the smartest thing he had ever done in his life. But he'd simply followed his instincts. Staring into Christina's beaming face, he knew he had done the right thing. She looked five years younger and ten times happier than he'd seen her for a long time. The worry lines that creased her brow and tugged her mouth down at the corners had vanished. The wary look that had haunted her during her divorce had been blown away just by the sight of Smokescreen running free.

She's not just pretty, Ben realised, she's beautiful.

The thought made him uncomfortable. There were many sexy women in the world so why was he falling for the one he couldn't have?

'Ben, you're not listening to me.' Christina had her hand on his arm. He imagined he could feel the heat of her touch even through the thick material of his jacket.

'Sorry.' She'd been talking and he hadn't heard a word.

'I asked if Smokie could run at Cheltenham.'

Ben gaped in disbelief. It was typical of her. A few weeks ago, they'd been thinking of retiring the horse. Now Christina was talking of running him at the Cheltenham Festival, the most demanding meeting in the jump-racing calendar.

'Tell you what,' he said. 'There's a race at Sandown on Saturday that will suit him fine.'

She frowned. 'But you've just seen him work. The Festival only comes once a year. Now's our chance.'

Ben had thought he might be able to head her off by mentioning Sandown. He tried again. 'It's a valuable race on Saturday. It would ease him back into competition and I don't think the field's that strong.'

'That's because the good horses will be at Cheltenham. And that's where Smokie belongs.'

Ben stared into her milky blue eyes. He was the trainer, the expert who knew the animals in his care inside out. When it came to horses, Ben was the boss. But not when it came to a woman like Christina Marcus.

'What did you have in mind?'

'The Gold Cup, of course.'

There are a handful of legendary steeplechases run around the world—the Grand National at Aintree, the Nakayama Grand Jump

5

in Japan, the gruelling Velka Pardubicka in the Czech Republic. These are tests of stamina and sheer good luck, as often as not won by the most fortunate. Luck rarely plays a big part in the winning of the Cheltenham Gold Cup. It is won by the best horse on the day. For the horse-racing followers and fans of the jumping game, the race itself *is* the best and prized above all others.

It was prized in particular by Alan Marcus, who had never won it and whose all-conquering steeplechaser Devil Moon was being prepared for the race in Ben's yard. Just now though he'd been among the pack left behind by Smokescreen.

Christina was staring at Ben, that soft kissable mouth now set in a thin impatient line. 'Well? Aren't you going to talk me out of it? Tell me I shouldn't put my horse up against Devil Moon?'

Ben would have tried if he thought he had any chance of succeeding.

But he could tell by the set of Christina's jaw and the determination in her eyes that there would be no point.

He ought to have been excited at the prospect of putting two good horses into the line-up of Cheltenham's most important race. But all he could see ahead was trouble.

'Cheer up.' Christina looped her arm through his as they walked back to his car and this time he didn't have the will-power to remove it. 'I'm dying to know how you've got Smokie back on form. You must be some kind of genius.'

If only he was.

CHAPTER TWO

Four years is a long time in the life of a racehorse—and in the life of a marriage. Four years ago, Ben had gone with Alan Marcus and his wife to Ireland. As ever, Alan was searching for a new horse to add to his string and Ben's job was to advise him. He knew what Alan was looking for—a young horse with the potential to make a top-class steeplechaser. One who could win a Gold Cup.

Ben had been on buying trips with Alan before but this was Christina's first time. The pair had been married for less than a year.

They flew to Shannon airport on the west coast and stayed at a hotel ten minutes from Limerick City. There was no shortage of horses to look at. Everyone in Ireland, from the taxi driver to the local postman, had an animal tucked away in a corner of a muddy field. And, funnily enough, all of these horses had the potential to become champions—according to their owners, at any rate.

After three days of gazing at

hopeless beasts, Ben was getting fed up. The rain didn't help, nor the fact that Alan appeared to blame him personally for their failure. Only Christina seemed unaffected. Though she didn't say much, she always found something to like about the useless animals paraded before them.

On their last afternoon, they finally found what they were looking for. As if on cue, the sun came out.

'That big black one there,' announced Alan as they looked into a paddock containing half a dozen frisky three-year-olds. 'He's the one I want.'

Ben had to give it to Alan. He had an eye for a horse all right, though he was inclined to be impulsive. The animal in question was a handsome creature. Even half-caked in mud he looked a picture of health, an athletic sort with a bold eye. He seemed older than the others, not just in looks but in behaviour.

A bale of hay had been cut open so all the horses could get at it. The black horse was keen to eat but not, it seemed, to share. When his companions lowered their heads to the hay, he shouldered them away.

Alan laughed. 'That's right, boy, you show 'em who's boss.'

'He's just a big bully,' said Christina.

Ben was surprised to hear her say so. It was the first time she'd disagreed with her husband in his hearing.

Alan turned to face her. 'You don't get anywhere in this world by being soft, sweetheart. That black one's a winner, the rest are also-rans as far as I'm concerned.'

As if to prove his point, the big horse charged at one of the others, his ears pinned back in fury as he chased his rival away from the food.

'There's more than one way to get what you want,' said Christina. 'Look at that one with the white face.'

10

A small chestnut was pulling happily at the hay while the black horse shooed the other animal off in a different direction.

'See,' she continued, 'that one gets to eat without having to throw his weight around. That's much more sensible, don't you think, Ben?'

The question took Ben by surprise. He didn't fancy getting caught between husband and wife.

But Alan wasn't letting him off the hook. 'Come on, Ben. Give us the benefit of your expensive opinion. Which one of those is most likely to win a race for me?'

It was a daft question, really. Ben knew that picking horses out in a field was like stepping into a classroom of children and selecting the bright ones on looks. In the end, successful horses were those with the talent and the heart to win. Neither quality was visible on the surface.

However, he'd had a quiet word with the breeder earlier. He was impressed by the pedigree of the two horses they were looking at.

'I'm with you on the black one,' he said to Alan. 'He's got a strong frame and he's aggressive. Those are great qualities in a racehorse.'

Alan grinned smugly at his wife. 'You see. I told you that was the horse to buy.'

It was the first time Ben really noticed the delicate pale blue of Christina's eyes. They were turned on him now, brimming with resentment.

But Ben hadn't finished. 'Christina's right about the other horse though. He's got a brain in his head and a clever horse can always find his way over a fence. Just because he looks cute doesn't mean he's not tough as well.'

'He's too damn small,' objected Alan.

Ben nodded. 'At the moment maybe. I reckon he'll be plenty big enough when he's filled out properly.'

'What are you saying?' Alan growled. 'That I should buy the brown one not the black?'

Ben was considering his reply when Christina slipped her arm round her husband's waist. 'No, darling. What he's saying is that you should buy them both—one for you and one for me.'

And, to Ben's astonishment, that's exactly what Alan did. Within a month, Devil Moon and Smokescreen, the bullying black horse and the white-faced chestnut, had started their lives in training in Ben's yard.

CHAPTER THREE

Ben's office was a poky little room with bare breezeblock walls and one small window without a curtain. All the same, it was big enough to hold a desk, a couple of chairs, an old TV, and a kettle that worked. It was a good place to get out of the raw March wind and take stock of what had taken place up on the gallops.

'Come on, Ben, I'm dying to hear how you did it.'

Christina was watching impatiently as the trainer poured boiling water into two mugs.

'Did what?' said Ben as he handed over her coffee.

'You know very well. Got Smokie back on form. The last time I came here he looked like he'd given up.'

The previous season Smokescreen had chipped a bone in his knee. It was his first injury but looked like no more than a setback. Ben had hoped the horse would mend over the summer in time for the serious contests of the winter. But Smokie's recovery was a long time coming, as he began to suffer from one niggle after another. By Boxing Day, when his stable mate Devil Moon was winning at Kempton, Smokescreen was still unfit to race. Some thought his career might be over.

The horse belonged to Alan in those days. He'd rung Ben and said, 'Is he ever going to race again? Yes or no?'

'I'm sure he will one day.'

'When's that going to be, then?'

'I can't say exactly.'

Alan had not been impressed. 'Just tell me one thing,' he'd demanded. 'Out of Devil Moon and Smokescreen, which one's more likely to win me the Cheltenham Gold Cup?'

There was no doubt. 'Devil Moon,' Ben had said, though it felt like a betrayal. He'd always had a soft spot for Smokie.

Shortly after that, ownership of the horse had passed into Christina's hands as part of her divorce settlement.

Despite all his efforts since, Ben had not been able to get the horse fit. He'd decided that Smokescreen's problem was seated between his big chestnut ears. Physically, the horse was in reasonable health but there was no spring in his step or sparkle in his eye. He picked at his food and was generally listless.

For the past month Christina had not been able to get to the yard— she'd been working in a play in Glasgow. In some respects, Ben had been pleased she'd stayed away. There would have been no fun for her in turning up to watch Smokie plodding lifelessly along the gallops. But things were different now.

He looked at her perching on the edge of his desk, as out of place in this shabby space as an orchid in a potato patch. Her thick honey-blonde hair tumbled to her shoulders. Her powder-blue sweater—cashmere, no doubt— matched her eyes. He had read in a gossip column she'd been seen in London nightspots with a hot young film director. Now that she was divorced from Alan, obviously she was not short of new admirers.

'Are you all right, Ben?' she said. 'You don't seem quite with it this morning.'

'I feel fine, thanks very much.'

Exasperation flashed across her face but she did not pursue it. 'OK, just tell me what you did to Smokie.'

He'd been delaying the moment. He wanted to make the most of it.

'Do you remember the grey mare I had here last summer?'

She grinned. 'Of course. Cupcakes. She was gorgeous. She had the box next to Smokie, didn't she?'

'Exactly. And when Smokie was getting over his injury I put her in the paddock with him for company. They spent all summer together.'

'So?'

'They became real friends.'

'How sweet.'

'Then, in January, Cupcakes did a leg and the owner decided to take

17

her home and breed from her.'

Ben could see the light dawning on Christina's face. 'January is when Smokie went off his food,' she said.

'He went off everything. Turned into a useless lump.'

'And it's because he was pining for Cupcakes?'

Ben nodded. 'I remember thinking at the time that I'd never seen horses so close. The funny thing was that they didn't mind being separated, until the day Cupcakes left for good. Then they screamed their heads off, as if they knew they wouldn't see each other again. It never crossed my mind that Smokie wouldn't get over it. A couple of weeks ago I was so desperate I got Cupcakes back. It was a last resort. She's getting free bed and board as long as it works out.'

'I bet it was some reunion,' she said.

'Not half. Smokie started screaming before Cupcakes had even got out of the horsebox. He almost knocked down his stable door to get at her.'

Christina's smile lit up the little room. 'It must be love.'

He smiled too. Her mood was infectious. 'Don't go marrying them off. Smokie's not able to have that kind of relationship.'

Like the majority of jump racehorses, Smokescreen had been gelded.

'I don't mean *that*.' The smile was gone from her face. 'I think real friendship is as much a part of love as sex, don't you?'

'What's wrong with both?' he said.

His words hung in the silence for a second.

'My feelings exactly,' she replied.

CHAPTER FOUR

Christina had to force herself to concentrate as she drove home from the yard. She was feeling so light-headed there was a danger she'd not notice if a ten-tonne truck pulled out ahead of her.

To think that Smokie had finally come back to health. And that he was in better form than ever. And that she could run him in the Gold Cup. It was more, far more, than she could ever have hoped for. And she had Ben to thank for it.

But she didn't want to think about Ben right now.

Contrary to most people's opinion, good looks are not always a blessing in life—at any rate, that was the conclusion Christina had come to. Her heart-shaped face and graceful step had singled her out for male attention from an early age. In the case of her stepfather, that attention had resulted in her leaving home as soon as she could. And there'd been plenty more men like creepy Gerald, eager to give her a helping hand. Provided, of course, she returned the favour.

When she'd managed to land a place at drama school, some said she'd only got in on her looks and even her friends assumed she'd have a brilliant career simply by cashing in on her beauty. But it hadn't worked out like that. The acting world was full of pretty girls with the self-belief to back it up. Christina did not have that kind of confidence. Though she believed in her talent, she did not assume that success was her destiny. And she wasn't about to hop into bed with a producer or a casting director on the promise of a part. She spent most of the two years after drama school out of work.

It had been a shock when she'd fallen in love. It hadn't been what she wanted. At the time, her career had just turned a corner—or so she thought. She had the promise of a decent part in a TV film on location in Ireland. To fill in time and earn some money she signed on with an agency which supplied hospitality girls to appear at sporting events. Her first booking was at Newbury racecourse, making sure the corporate customers in private boxes had everything they needed to enjoy their day.

Dressed in a black skirt, white blouse and a scarlet jacket with a nipped-in waist, her job was to fetch drinks, place bets for the clients— and to smile. Good humour was required, no matter what. She didn't think it would be hard, even as the men around her loosened their ties and their tongues and began a serious assault on the stocks of alcohol. She wasn't bothered. She was at home in the company of boozy gamblers—they reminded her of her real father.

On this occasion, one man went too far, demanding her attention, angling for her phone number, joking about whisking her off for a weekend in Paris. Except Christina didn't think it was a joke. She placed bets for him, bigger ones as the afternoon wore on. He claimed she brought him luck. But the luck ran out on the last race and his temper turned in the face of her smiling refusals. She wondered why he had switched to red wine for his last drink of the afternoon until he tipped it all down her blouse.

'So sorry, darling,' he said. 'Let me help you out of your wet things.'

She was going to hit him, an open-palmed slap across his smirking face and to hell with the job, but suddenly he wasn't there to hit. A man in a dark suit had stepped between them and, in one movement it seemed, bundled her abuser away. His protests were cut off as the door slammed shut behind them.

When Christina emerged from the toilet—one of the other girls had magically supplied a spare blouse— her rescuer was waiting for her, full of apologies. He was tall, with a long thin face and slender white fingers that took hers gently. She saw again the way he had descended like a black cloud on her tormentor, those fingers seizing the other man in a grip he couldn't break. Deep-set eyes of grey shone into hers as if he was looking for something. This wasn't a man who would be impressed simply by the surface of things. Mere good looks would not be enough for Alan Marcus.

It was a while before she found out who he was—one of the wealthiest men in the country—and she didn't much care anyway. Big business and boardroom power didn't interest her in the slightest. And he seemed to like that in her. She wasn't impressed by his riches and he saw beyond her beauty. They were a perfect match.

All that changed in time, of course. She hadn't given him what he wanted, whatever that was— complete submission, she suspected. He was an empire builder and he wanted her to run the domestic side of his empire. The job was too big for her, she'd decided. When you teamed up with someone whose ambitions were vast it left no room for your own, modest though they might be. What was the point of taking small parts in plays that earned her nothing when she could paper the walls with Alan's money? To Christina, of course, there was plenty of point but her husband was dismissive. As Mrs Marcus, she was allowed no dreams of her own.

Well, that was behind her now. She did not regret loving Alan, though she knew he did not feel the same way. He acted as if she was now his enemy. She supposed that was the way he coped with the failure of their marriage. After all, he wasn't used to losing.

CHAPTER FIVE

News travels fast in the small world of horse racing. Smokescreen's return to form on the Lambourn gallops did not remain secret for long.

Alan Marcus was sitting in the boardroom of an office in Canary Wharf when the mobile in his jacket rang loudly. This was his private number, the one he gave to the girls he bedded and his racing informants. Without regard to the meeting taking place around him—a young woman in glasses and a business suit was talking—he took the phone from his pocket.

A dozen pairs of eyes stared at him. The talks were in their second day, with two teams of executives wading clause by clause through an agreement designed to merge their two companies. Most of those present were lawyers. By agreement, all of them had switched off their phones but not Alan, the most important person in the room. As far as he was concerned, there was one law for him and the rest could stuff it. Their resentment was written on their faces.

Alan peered at the number on the small screen. 'Carry on without me,' he announced as he jumped to his feet.

In fact, the deal they were discussing was less of a merger than a takeover—and Alan was taking over. Thimbles, the small West Country chain of convenience stores, would fit sweetly into A&M, his national supermarket conglomerate. Thimbles controlled some prime locations, ripe either for expansion or conversion to A&M Village Corners, high-street versions of the

A&M superstores. A proportion of the Thimbles shop-floor staff could be retained, together with a few of the brighter head-office personnel.

As for the rest of Thimbles, they could take their chances in the job market. There was no room for sentiment in business. The precise number of redundancies was the point at issue when his mobile captured Alan's attention.

'You can't leave right now,' said the woman who had been speaking. She was a member of the Thimbles legal team and by far the smartest in Alan's opinion.

'Don't get your knickers in a twist, Ms Hurst,' he said.

Behind the lenses of her spectacles, her eyes flashed with anger. Big green eyes, Alan noticed, shaped like almonds.

The others just sat there as spineless as jellyfish. Hurst was worth the lot of them put together.

'Be back shortly,' he said and

strode through the door.

In a room on the next floor overlooking the river, Alan returned the call. As he waited irritably for an answer, he did not notice the lazy grey snake of the Thames at his feet or think of the room full of people below waiting for him to rule on their future. He thought only of Devil Moon, his brilliant black steeplechaser who was destined to win the Cheltenham Gold Cup in a few days' time.

Unless there was a problem.

Liam, his caller, was a lad who worked at Ben Sayers' yard. Alan paid him to be his eyes and ears in the stables and keep him informed— and not just about his own animals.

So many things could go wrong with horses. They could easily go lame or start to cough or trip over their own feet. In Alan's opinion, which he expressed often, horses were more delicate than women. And, God knows, a female only had to break a fingernail to flounce off to her bedroom and cry for a whole day. He'd owned some horses just like that. But surely not Devil Moon.

'Is the Devil OK?' he barked down the phone when Liam finally answered.

'Yeah, don't worry. He's in tip-top nick. No worries.'

Good.

'So why are you calling me?'

'I thought you should know that Smokescreen did a decent bit of work this morning.'

'Smokescreen? I thought he was past it.'

'Not this morning, he wasn't. He fair burned up the gallop. Left Devil Moon and the rest of 'em for dead.'

Alan took this in. It was galling to think that after all this time Smokescreen had finally come back to form and he no longer owned him. Christina had made a special plea for Smokie as part of the divorce settlement on the grounds that she'd spotted him in the first place. Alan had agreed—it had looked like the horse's career was over—but now he regretted the decision. He should never have let the animal go.

'That's excellent news,' he forced himself to say. 'I'm obliged to you, Liam.'

'There's more, Mr Marcus. The word is that they're going to run Smokie in the Gold Cup.'

Liam's words had the force of an unexpected punch in the gut.

'Are you sure?'

'Dead sure. The lad who looks after him told me. It'll be in all the papers tomorrow.'

'But—' Alan cast around for a reason why this grim news should be false—'that horse hasn't raced all season. A burn-up on a gallop's one thing but it's sheer stupidity to put him straight into the Gold Cup. It's the toughest race of the year.'

'Between you and me, I think that's the boss's opinion too but

Mrs Marcus is insisting.'

Well, she would and Alan knew why. The mention of his ex-wife brought a sour taste to his mouth. She'd love to rob him of the one prize in racing he desired above all others.

Alan cut off the call without saying goodbye.

Bloody Christina. He'd picked her to share his life. Welcomed her into a world of wealth she could only have dreamed of. But she'd not kept her side of the bargain. As if looking decorative and making a home was that hard! She'd refused even to consider giving up work to have a family.

Alan knew a bit of history. He realised how Henry VIII must have felt when Anne Boleyn turned out to be rotten. If only he could put his ex-wife's head on the block.

Even he, with all his wealth and power, could not do that. But maybe he could do the next best thing and scupper the chances of her horse.

CHAPTER SIX

Ben took the call from Christina in the kitchen as he was fixing himself supper. He wasn't much of a cook but he could fry a sausage.

She wanted to know about Smokie—was he all right after his work that morning? She sounded anxious. After the horse's long lay-off it was only natural.

Ben put her mind at ease. Smokie was fine. He told her he'd booked Charlie Stubbs, an experienced jockey, to ride him at Cheltenham. Other than that, there was no news.

He thought she'd ring off then but she didn't. She told him the London evening paper was carrying the story of Smokescreen's entry into the Gold Cup reckoning. That was no real surprise.

'I don't suppose you've heard from Alan,' she said. 'About Smokie, I mean.'

Ben knew very well what she meant. There was an eagerness in her tone. She was keen to know how her ex had reacted.

'No,' said Ben. 'I haven't heard from him all day.'

In the background, Ben heard a man's voice calling her and felt a stab of jealousy. It was ridiculous.

'He's going to be hopping mad when he hears about it,' she said.

The voice called again, something about being late for dinner.

'And if Smokie wins,' she went on cheerfully, 'he'll be pig sick. I'd love to see his face.'

Smoke drifted across the kitchen. Ben's sausages were burning.

'Look, Christina, I've got to go.'

'Me, too. I'm running late. I'll speak to you tomorrow.'

He stirred his spoilt supper morosely, picturing Christina dolled up for the evening on the arm of her boyfriend. He tried to put the image out of his head. He wasn't in her league. He was a fool to care about her.

A fool to care about telling her a lie.

Of course Alan had spoken to him about Smokie. The businessman had been on the phone within a couple of hours of the decision to run Christina's horse at Cheltenham.

'Naturally, I'm delighted to hear that Smokescreen is on the mend,' Alan had said. He hadn't sounded delighted. 'But you can't seriously intend to put him up against Devil Moon.'

'It's what Christina wants.'

'She's only entering the Gold Cup to spite me. You know that, don't you?'

'I don't think so,' he'd said with more conviction than he'd felt. 'Anybody is entitled to try and win it if they've got a good enough horse.'

'Then let me remind you that you told me Devil Moon was the better horse. More likely to win the Gold Cup than Smokescreen, you said.'

'That's what I believed at the time.' Ben hadn't been able to deny it.

'And I took your word for it. You're the expert, after all. But if Smokescreen wins, I'm going to find it hard to trust you in the future.' He paused for a moment to let the implied threat sink in, then added, 'On the other hand, if you were right about Devil Moon a bonus would be in order. I'm thinking of splitting the prize money with you fifty-fifty. That's a lot of money.'

It was indeed. There was a lot Ben could do with £100,000. He could pay off the overdraft for a start. It would be good finally to be working for himself and not the bank. He could also lay a new all-weather surface or build some new stables. And there ought to be some money left over for a few treats, like an evening in a fine restaurant with a woman he cared for by his side.

There was only one woman he cared for and she was off-limits— unless he wanted to make a lifelong enemy of the man who had promised to wipe out his debts.

He chucked his burnt food into the bin.

CHAPTER SEVEN

Alan Marcus opened his eyes in the half-light of dawn. He was instantly wide awake and bad-tempered. The rhythmic call of a wood pigeon in the tree outside his bedroom echoed in his head like the beat of a drum. He knew he wouldn't get back to sleep.

The woman by his side still slumbered soundly as he slipped out of bed.

In the kitchen, Alan made himself

tea, leaving the tea bag in a brown puddle on the draining board. The housekeeper could clear it up later.

He sat in the gloom of the living room, a room that didn't see much living. On the occasions he stayed in his Kensington town house he preferred the snug next door where he ate TV dinners on a comfy old sofa. Now though he stared out over the misty lawns and neat shrubs of the garden, probing the causes of his discontent.

His sleep had been ended by a dream. A dream so vivid it seemed to play over in his mind's eye.

He was at Cheltenham racecourse on Gold Cup day, watching the race with a glass of champagne in his hand. Devil Moon had just cruised into the lead with two fences left to jump. His rivals were flagging and Smokescreen was nowhere. His heart lifted. This was going to be the easiest Gold Cup victory in living memory.

Then he was in a scrum of people, beery oafs and shrieking women waving betting slips in the air. He was trying to get to the winner's enclosure for the presentation but the crowd were blocking his way. Worse than that, he didn't know for certain that Devil Moon had won. He'd not seen the end of the race, or else he could not recall it and no one would tell him. But the Devil had been so far ahead, surely victory must have been his.

The crowd parted suddenly and he could see that the prize-giving was about to take place. People clapped and cheered. He could see Ben on the rostrum shaking hands with a man in a suit. Ben Sayers—Devil Moon's trainer. So he must have won. Thank God. The cheers were for him.

But they weren't. The smiles and applause were for his ex-wife, Christina, who was mounting the rostrum to accept the cup. In the way of dreams, she was wearing the extravagant white dress she was married in. Cradling the trophy in her arms, she turned to him and smiled in triumph.

The worst of it was that his father was standing by his side. 'She's holding that cup like a baby,' he said. 'Pity she never gave you one.'

'Don't start, Dad.'

'Every man needs a son. Like you and me, eh?'

'Belt up, you old bastard.'

'Never mind, son. I know you're upset about the race but there's always next year.' As ever, his father had a cheery cliché to hand when things went wrong, which, in his case, was often. 'You surprised me by letting Christina have that horse though. Not like you, Alan.'

*　　　*　　　*

Alan put down his empty cup and shook his head, trying to rid himself of that familiar, irritating tone—the tone that had shaped his entire life. His father had been dead fifteen years but the old fellow was still on his back.

He told himself he had bettered everything his father had ever done in business. Dad had been too soft, reluctant to take the hard decisions. He should have dumped his partners and sold out when there was money on the table. Instead, he was the one who had got shafted.

The only place Alan had not bested his old man was the racecourse. His father had won the Gold Cup when Alan was six and had taken the boy with him up onto the rostrum to receive the prize. Standing there, basking in the applause of the crowd, Alan had boasted to his father that one day he would win the cup too. 'I hope you do, son,' his dad had said, 'and if you do, you'll have earned it.' The boy had wondered what he'd meant by that.

But he would win it. This year. The dream had only one significance—he could do more to make sure of victory.

Everything in the end came down to the power of money.

CHAPTER EIGHT

'Alan.'

The voice came from behind him, interrupting his train of thought.

He turned to see his companion from the night before standing in the doorway. She was half-dressed in a slip, her hair falling in a copper curtain down to her shoulders.

'You're up early,' he said.

She'd instructed him to call her Tilly, short for Matilda. But he preferred to think of her simply as Hurst.

'I've called a cab,' she said. 'I need

to go home and change.'

He nodded, thinking that he'd never noticed her clothes before but he would now. Hurst without her business armour—the suit, the glasses, the hairpins—was a different creature. Last night she had been soft, submissive, yielding—all that a woman should be in his opinion.

There had been no submission from her at the beginning though. She'd found Alan in his office at the end of the previous afternoon. The merger talks had ground on all day with the main issue—the number of redundancies—unresolved. His absence from the meeting for half of the time had not helped.

Hurst had taken him by surprise, bursting into the room just as he was hunting in the office fridge for soda that wasn't flat.

'I want a word, Mr Marcus.'

He could see that she was bottling up a whole torrent of them. Her cheeks were flushed and her small pointed chin thrust accusingly at him. She looked a bit like his ex-wife, Christina, when she was bent on picking a fight. Did all these witches come out of the same coven?

He leaned back in his chair. 'Spit it out then.'

'I was looking forward to seeing you in action, Mr Marcus. Seeing first-hand how a successful man conducts his business. I can't tell you how disillusioned and outraged I am.'

'Do try, Ms Hurst.'

'You're just a bully. An arrogant, thick-skinned, woman-hating despot who puts his own selfish pleasures above other people's basic welfare.'

'This is your considered opinion, is it?'

'Do you deny that you care less about the future of hundreds of Thimbles employees than you do about the result of a horse race?'

He'd been surprised at that. He'd

not discussed the issue of the Gold Cup with anyone in the office. She'd obviously done her homework on him.

She placed her hands on his desk and leaned forward to glare into his face.

'If you don't give me a guarantee on jobs, Mr Marcus, I shall be praying that Devil Moon breaks his neck.'

'Pray all you like, my dear, it won't make any difference to the horse.'

'Smokescreen can beat him.'

'Smokescreen has been out of action for over a year.'

'So? He's beaten Devil Moon before, hasn't he? In a bumper at Market Rasen.'

For once Alan was lost for words. He was amazed this girl even knew what a bumper was—a race for jump horses run over the flat.

'That was two years ago,' he snapped. 'Devil Moon was a total novice. It was his first time on a racecourse.'

'It was Smokescreen's first race too, wasn't it?'

Damn the woman. She was grinning. Smokescreen was one way to get under his skin.

He took the bottle from his desk drawer. He wasn't going to wait for a drink any longer.

'Take a seat,' he grunted. 'I've only got whisky.'

'I don't think I should be drinking with you.'

'Why not? All your deadbeat colleagues will be knocking it back in a wine bar on the wharf. Sit down. I want to set you straight about horses.'

'What about jobs, Mr Marcus? The Thimbles staff you're so keen to throw on the scrapheap.'

He sighed heavily as he lined up two glasses. 'All right, Ms Hurst, we'll discuss jobs too if that will keep you happy. As it happens, there is some room for manoeuvre on that point. Just park your arse.'

'You're also foul-mouthed and vulgar,' she said as she sat. 'I forgot to mention that earlier.'

He ignored the remark. 'Soda?'

'I like it neat.'

Of course she did and she could put it away too.

Her father was a bookie so that explained how she knew about horses. Her mum had died young and her dad had gone bankrupt so that explained her bleeding heart.

He guaranteed a hundred Thimbles jobs. He could always give more later.

She threw some light on an area of the Thimbles accounts that was less than transparent. She could tell him more too, he was certain.

It was a damn sight more productive dealing one on one with the opposition than being cooped up with a crowd of them all day.

Evidently she thought so too because when he suggested they put some food in their stomachs she'd agreed. With the Bentley in the garage and a driver on hand to take them back to his apartment in Kensington, it seemed the obvious next step. Alan knew a very superior takeaway food service. He'd let her order.

He'd made the pass in the car on the way back. Though alcohol-inspired, it was a calculated risk. After all, he could hardly sink lower in her estimation.

But she'd not rejected him. Her mouth tasted of the drinks they'd shared. Whisky kisses. They reminded him of his youth, when he'd seduced secretaries in his office after hours.

She'd called him a lecherous sod but she'd stayed the night all the same. And now she had the sense to take herself off. It wouldn't suit either of them to arrive at the office together.

'Look,' she said. 'We can forget this ever happened. It doesn't change a thing.'

By which Alan assumed she meant she would be just as combative an opponent in the office today as she had been yesterday. But it did change things. That was the point of it.

He put his hand on her shoulder, her almost-bare shoulder where the fall of her hair skimmed the warm skin. 'I'm busy tonight but how about tomorrow? A proper dinner.'

She blinked. With pleasure, maybe, or gratitude or some other emotion he couldn't read. He didn't know her that well. Not yet.

'Possibly,' she said.

CHAPTER NINE

That evening Alan drove himself to Lambourn. There was no need to trouble the chauffeur. The fewer people who knew about this visit to

Ben's yard the better.

As he drove, he did not think about Thimbles or the meeting that had swallowed up his day or even the green eyes of Matilda Hurst. He thought about how much he resented his former wife.

All told, from courtship to divorce court, their relationship had lasted six years. And what had he got out of it? Some hot romance at the beginning, granted, but you didn't have to marry a girl to get that. It was also true that Christina had always looked good on his arm at business functions and race meetings. But no one got married for a slinky piece of arm candy. Glamorous companions were ten a penny for a man with his wealth.

As for what Christina had not given him, the list was long but could be summed up in one word— commitment. Complete commitment to his company was what he required of all his employees, and complete commitment to him was the least he expected of his wife. But Christina hadn't even taken charge of his homes. With the London and Sussex houses, the flat in Monte Carlo, the apartment in New York—and the staff that went with them—there was more than enough to keep her occupied. But she had insisted on pursuing her so-called acting career, which was a joke. A role as a dying drug addict in *Casualty* was not the stepping stone to an Academy Award, in Alan's opinion.

And she had refused to give him children. That was the bottom line. What was the point of building a business dynasty if he didn't have a son to leave it to?

'Not yet,' she'd said. Not ever, he'd concluded after she'd kept him waiting for five years. Then he found himself looking at other women, girls more likely to fall in with his plans. On reflection, it was as well he and Christina didn't have kids to tie them together. Now he'd paid her off, there could be a complete break. She'd now got more money than she could ever hope to earn in a career of bit-part TV appearances.

Except that Christina wouldn't go away. She must have got herself a new press agent, because her face was all over the papers these days. The divorce had drawn a fair amount of coverage and she was using that to keep her name in the public eye. She was probably after some film role.

He could shrug the matter off but today she had been featured on the back pages as well. Smokescreen's surprise entry for the Gold Cup had proved a good excuse to run her picture in the sports coverage. Some respected racing journalists were even enthusiastic about Smokie's chances at Cheltenham, despite his long lay-off. It made Alan's blood boil.

He'd phoned ahead to make sure Ben would be at home. The trainer was standing in the door of the old farmhouse as Alan parked in the yard and took his briefcase from the boot.

He turned down Ben's offer of a drink and listened to the trainer's quick report on Devil Moon's condition without response. He was here to say his piece and leave.

They faced each other in the front room. Chairs were arranged neatly round a heavy rosewood dining table. It had an air of being rarely used.

Alan placed his briefcase on the table.

'I've been thinking about our conversation the other day,' he said. 'I hope I made it clear how generous I am prepared to be to see Devil Moon win the Gold Cup.'

A smile seemed to tug at Ben's lips. Then it was quickly suppressed. 'It's OK, Alan. You don't have to promise me half the prize money. I'm going to do my best for your horse anyway.'

Alan was irritated. Obviously the trainer thought he was trying to go back on his word.

'The offer still stands—we split the purse if the Devil wins. That's not why I'm here.'

Alan snapped open the clips of the briefcase. 'I've got another incentive in mind. As you know, I'm not happy that Smokescreen is running in the race. It's a sore point—for reasons you can appreciate.'

Ben said nothing, just stared at him. There was no hint of a smile now.

'Whatever happens in the race to Devil Moon,' said Alan, 'I don't want Smokescreen to win. Any horse but him, do you understand?'

'I understand, Alan, but it's a race. It's what happens on the day.'

'I don't accept that. You're the trainer. You can stop Smokescreen if you want to.'

Ben was annoyed. 'My job is to get

horses to the start in the best possible condition. After that, it's out of my hands.'

'Bollocks,' said Alan and opened the briefcase. The banknotes were in bags but their values were visible through the plastic, bundles of ten-pound and twenty-pound notes. He could see the trainer staring. That was good. He'd never known a naked display of hard cash to fail.

'People in my business,' Alan said, 'can pull off miracles if there's a big enough carrot dangling under their noses. And this, my friend, is your carrot.'

The trainer opened his mouth to speak but Alan stopped him.

'I never want to see this money again. I don't care what you do with it. Just make sure Smokescreen does not win that race.'

He left without saying goodbye.

On the drive back to London Alan planned the phone call he would make the next day. If there was one thing he had learned in business, you could never have too much insurance.

*   *   *

Ben listened to Alan's car disappearing down the drive, his gaze still on the open case on the table.

Racing folk can be casual about money. At the racecourse, Ben was used to seeing wads of banknotes changing hands, spilling out of old wallets or stuffed into a back pocket. On rare occasions, he'd had a 'present' from an owner after a good day—an envelope bulging with folding cash. He'd once seen a successful punter toss a handful of his winnings up into the air and laugh as the notes covered his drunken pals like autumn leaves.

But he'd never seen as much money as this. New notes, crisply stacked and wrapped—it was impossible to say how much.

Alan had said Ben could stop Smokescreen if he wanted to and he'd denied it. But he could. All he had to do was remove Cupcakes, and Smokie would become the listless, miserable animal he had been before. He'd be beaten before he even lined up at Cheltenham.

It would be that simple.

CHAPTER TEN

The restaurant was light and airy. Even though it was busy, it did not seem crowded. Each table seemed to exist in its own ocean of space. Alan had chosen it carefully. He very much wanted to please his dinner guest.

Matilda Hurst had laid aside her business clothes for the evening. She wore a loose linen jacket over an oyster pale blouse and her hair hung free. She looked a different creature to his boardroom opponent. Not that her opposition had seemed so fierce these past two days. Her negotiating style had been much less tigerish since their night together. Alan had known her seduction would turn out to be a good move.

Whatever the reason, the merger discussion had passed off much more smoothly and agreement had finally been reached. All that remained was the secretarial chore of preparing the final contract, which Alan expected to sign when he returned from the Cheltenham Festival.

He raised his glass of champagne. He didn't much care for the stuff but he'd ordered it anyway. It was expected on occasions like this.

'Congratulations, Tilly,' he said. He was coming to terms with the name.

'What for?'

'You've done a splendid job. I'd have wiped the floor with your lot if it wasn't for you. Now we've got a deal we can all celebrate.'

Her mouth turned down at the corners. 'Actually, I think you did wipe the floor with us.'

She was right. There was no soft-soaping this woman.

'Three hundred Thimbles people are going to end up out of work,' she said. 'I don't think that's anything to celebrate.'

'It would have been more than that if it wasn't for you. Believe me, you did the best you could.'

'I suppose.' Finally she sipped from her glass and her face relaxed. 'I find it hard to walk away sometimes.'

Hurst wasn't a Thimbles staff member. She worked for a City law firm which offered advice on the buying and selling of businesses. Her specialist area was the retail sector— hence her use to the West Country

59

firm. So her own job was safe, whatever happened to her friends at Thimbles.

'What are you up to next?' Alan asked.

She shrugged. 'I'm not sure. A holiday maybe. Actually, I'm thinking of changing careers.'

'To do what?'

'I might retrain as a teacher.'

'Why?' Alan was puzzled. A woman in her position would be making decent money. She would also be well placed to jump on board one of her client companies at a senior level if she played her cards right.

'I've been helping fat cats like you wheel and deal for too long. Now I'd like to do something else.'

'Like be a teacher?' Alan tried to keep the distaste out of his voice. He couldn't imagine anything worse.

'I'd like to do something with children since I'm not likely to have any of my own.'

He absorbed the statement. 'Why on earth not?'

'I just have a feeling. My taste in men is terrible, for a start.' She flashed him an impudent grin.

'Like me, you mean?'

'Well, you are a foul-mouthed chauvinist bully.'

'Why are you here, then?' he said.

'Why did you ask me?' she replied.

That was a good question but, before he could answer it, waiters appeared with their food and the moment passed.

Later, after they'd finished with wine and had moved on to brandy, he invited her to accompany him to Cheltenham.

'I don't know,' she said. 'Sounds a bit dangerous to me.'

'What do you mean?'

'I'm not sure I want to be anywhere near you when your ex-wife's horse beats yours.'

He'd nearly exploded there and then, slamming his glass down so the pale liquid lurched around the bowl. 'Don't even bloody joke about it,' he growled.

'You see? You're not a good loser, are you, Alan?'

He forced a smile on to his face. She had a point.

'Sorry, Tilly,' he said and noticed the surprise on her face. She'd probably not heard him apologise before. Not many people had. 'If you come with me, I promise to behave myself.'

She sipped her drink and eyed him shrewdly. 'I've got money on Smokescreen, you know. I think he's going to stroll home.'

'I hope you haven't bet much. It's money down the drain.'

'Says you. He's beaten Devil Moon before and he's a much better price. Actually, I'm thinking of putting more on.'

'Don't be a fool.'

'Come off it, Alan. Just because I disagree with you doesn't make me a fool. I think Smokescreen is the best horse.'

He sighed. 'It's not a matter of opinion. It's a fact. Smokescreen can't win.'

'Can't?' She eyed him shrewdly. 'Or won't?'

He caught the waiter's eye and asked for the bill, letting her question hang in the air unanswered.

'So,' he said finally, 'are you coming to Cheltenham with me, or not?'

She nodded her head. 'Yes, please.'

That was more like it.

CHAPTER TEN

Christina Marcus was finding it difficult to get to sleep—but that wasn't unusual. Sleep had been hard to come by during the agonies of her divorce. Once, she'd be out like a light when her head touched the pillow but not any more. Now she lay awake chewing over Smokie's chances at Cheltenham and wondering whether to pack in her acting career. And she was thinking about Ben.

She was surprised when the phone rang. Who could it be at one in the morning?

She didn't recognise the voice.

'You don't know me, so don't ask.' It was a woman. 'I'm calling about your horse Smokescreen.'

Oh God. Smokie. 'Is there something wrong?'

'No. Well, not exactly. I'm not sure how to put this . . .'

Christina decided to hang up. This was a crank call. But she still held the receiver to her ear as the woman continued.

'Do you trust your trainer, Mrs Marcus?'

'Absolutely.'

'I don't think you should be so sure

of him. He trains your husband's horses too, doesn't he?'

'So what?'

There was silence on the line. Hang up now, Christina told herself, but she held on.

'I just wanted to warn you. Ben's not got a big yard, has he? Can he afford to let Smokescreen win?'

The call was cut off.

Christina replaced the receiver and turned on the light. She definitely would not be going to sleep now.

What a horrible thing. Some mean-spirited cow ringing her in the middle of the night to make stupid accusations. She must have seen the pictures of her and Smokie in the paper. Some people were weird.

But how had she got this phone number? Maybe it wasn't hard to find, through her agent or off the internet.

Anyway, why say such things? If it wasn't for Ben, Smokie wouldn't be fit to race at all.

But Ben hadn't wanted Smokie to go to Cheltenham.

And he had been acting strangely when he was with her. Not meeting her eye and being reluctant to speak his mind—as if he were nursing a secret.

And—she sat up, suddenly rigid with fear—he could easily stop Smokie from running his best in the Gold Cup.

Ben didn't have to harm the horse or interfere with him in any way. All he had to do was remove Cupcakes.

Christina was dressed and out of the house in under three minutes.

*   *   *

If he were honest, Ben would admit that he had sometimes dreamed of being woken in the middle of the night by Christina Marcus knocking on his door. But this Christina was not the smiling vision of his dreams.

Her eyes were hard and unfriendly.

'I want to see Smokescreen.'

'At this hour?'

'I want to see him.'

He'd dressed hastily, pulling on jeans and a T-shirt to answer the door. Now he looked for his boots and grabbed a sweater while she waited impatiently.

'What's this all about, Christina?'

'Just hurry up.'

He'd never seen her like this before. She was an angry woman and her anger was bitter and cold. As if she had caught him in an act of betrayal.

He gave up trying to talk to her and led her round the house and into the stable, first keying in his security code at the outside door, then unlocking the inside gate. Precautions were tight in the yard, particularly at this point of the season. He'd installed two new CCTV cameras in the past month.

Animals stirred in their boxes at

their approach.

'They think it's an early start,' he said.

She ignored the remark.

What was this about? Did she know something he didn't? Was there a danger to the horse?

They reached Smokescreen's stall and Ben shone his torch inside. A big shape stirred and ambled over to the door. A familiar horsey face blinked back at them.

'See—he's fine.'

Christina looked different in the half-light, the angles of her face sharp, all softness gone. 'Where's Cupcakes?' she spat.

He directed the torch into the next stall. A small grey horse shifted in its beam, her head on one side as if she were about to ask a question.

'She's right here, wondering what the fuss is all about. Just like me.'

Christina didn't say anything, just looked backwards and forwards between the two horses, separated by the dividing wall of the stall. Then she hung her head. It was almost comical, as if she were a penitent child.

'Oh God,' she mumbled.

*　　　*　　　*

Ben made tea for them both in the kitchen. It was four in the morning. Too late for him to go back to bed. He was due in the yard at five thirty.

Christina had not explained herself and he'd not pressed her for an explanation. He didn't really care what had brought her banging on his door in the middle of the night. He'd known owners behave in the oddest ways in the days before a big race. Whatever it was, he was glad she had come.

Only one thing bothered him.

'Won't your new boyfriend be wondering where you are?'

She looked shocked, as if his words made no sense. Her surprise cheered him but he reminded himself that she was an actress.

'What did you say?'

He repeated himself.

'Where did you get the idea I had a new boyfriend?'

'I read the papers, Christina. Anyway, I heard him when you were on the phone to me the other night, telling you to hurry up.'

'Ah.' She put her mug down. 'What's it to you anyway?'

He shrugged. 'I just assumed. It's not my business. Sorry.'

She stared at him with an expression he couldn't read. 'Since I split up with Alan I've steered clear of boyfriends, as you put it. I'm friendly with lots of men and close to none. Except Stephen.'

Stephen? The film director in the paper had been called Conrad.

'Stephen,' she continued, 'is my brother. That's who you heard when I called you. He's a bit of a bossy sod.'

Relief tingled in his veins. Her brother.

'And then,' she added, 'there's you.'

'What about me?'

'I don't know. I thought you were my friend but maybe I'm just one of your clients. You've been very distant with me recently.'

Had he? He supposed he'd been trying to cover up how he felt about her.

'Tonight, I got a phone call. Someone suggested it might not be in your interest for Smokie to run well in the Gold Cup. Then I realised that all you had to do was take Cupcakes away.'

Indeed. And he'd been tempted— but he didn't say so.

Her face was dark. 'I'm sorry, Ben. I didn't want to believe it but I had to see for myself.'

Suddenly it was clear to Ben what he must do about Christina. And the money, sitting untouched in the

71

briefcase where Alan had left it.

She pushed her chair back and got to her feet. 'I'd better go,' she said.

He stopped her, his hands on her shoulders, his lips inches from hers.

'No, you don't,' he said and kissed her.

It was the moment he'd dreamed of, after all.

CHAPTER TWELVE

Alan eyed the man on the other side of the desk with suspicion. Henderson, his doctor for the last nine years, rarely looked pleased. He was a gloomy soul as a rule, especially when reading the results of a patient's blood tests.

'There's nothing to complain about here,' the doctor said. 'Even the cholesterol's down. I'd say you're in fine fettle.' He laughed. He had a habit of making references to horses before asking for a racing tip.

Alan reflected for a moment. It's true he was feeling good for once. The Thimbles business had worked out well. He was sleeping through the night once more. And the prospect of tomorrow's Gold Cup and all the gut-wrenching tension that went with it just filled him with excitement.

Liam's latest piece of news from Ben's yard had made him very happy. They'd spoken that morning and his informer had given a glowing account of Devil Moon's condition.

'I tell you, Mr Marcus, he'll be a picture in the parade ring. The best-looking horse there, I guarantee it.'

'Anything else?' Alan had snapped, the Gold Cup not being a beauty contest.

'Well, it's not really my business but—Mrs Marcus drives a Fiesta, doesn't she?'

'The last I heard.'

'There's been a red Fiesta parked

overnight in the yard for the past two nights. Not that I've actually seen her, mind. It's got a bashed-up wing mirror.'

So Christina hadn't got her car fixed. It didn't surprise Alan—she didn't care about things like that.

It didn't even surprise him that she and Ben were shacking up together. They'd got on well ever since that trip to Ireland. And when Alan had hired a private detective to spy on her before the divorce he'd half-expected to see Ben Sayers' name in the report. But Ben hadn't featured—no one had.

No, the biggest surprise of all, and it struck Alan forcibly as he sat in Henderson's Harley Street consulting room, was that he didn't much care who his ex-wife was sleeping with. Unless it had a bearing on how the Gold Cup turned out. But the way he'd fixed things he didn't see how it could.

Shag who you like, sweetheart, he

thought, I'll still come out on top.

'I don't mind telling you I was a little concerned last year.' Henderson shook his head. He could only be a couple of years older than Alan but he enjoyed playing the father figure. 'Divorce can be a severe test to physical and mental well-being, but you appear to have survived the ordeal without a scratch.'

'I suppose so.'

'In which case, Alan, I'm inclined to ask, what's her name?'

'Eh?'

'In my experience the most likely reason is that you've found another woman. What's her name?'

For a moment Alan was dumbfounded but he quickly recovered. 'If you must know, it's not a woman, it's a horse. Devil Moon's a certainty for the Gold Cup tomorrow.'

Henderson was all ears, hunting for a pen and paper. 'You're sure he's going to win?'

'As sure as an owner ever can be.'

'Excellent. Devil Moon, you said.' The doctor made a note. He'd got his tip.

Alan left the room feeling shaken. In answer to Henderson's question about a woman he'd nearly said, 'Matilda Hurst.'

CHAPTER THIRTEEN

For jump-racing fans, the Cheltenham Festival is the greatest occasion of the year. During the four days of the event, some 170,000 of them swarm all over the stands and enclosures. They encircle the parade ring to watch the horses strut before the races, thrust themselves into bars and restaurants, and mob the Tote windows and bookmakers' pitches in their eagerness to place a bet. By the time the Gold Cup comes round, anticipation is at fever pitch. In the jam-packed stands, a man could faint just breathing in the excitement. And if he should do so, a dozen kind strangers would catch him before he hit the ground.

A mile away, up on the highest part of the course, no such kindness softened the impact for jockey Charlie Stubbs as he hit the ground. He lay with his face in the grass, moisture from the wet turf seeping into his racing breeches. He didn't know where he was. The roaring in his ears meant something though. He must be riding at a meeting with a heck of a crowd.

He opened his eyes. The sky was a muddy grey, full of rain. Ahead, further down the slope, was a line of hurdles and beyond lay an undulating landscape that he recognised in an instant. Now he realised what must have happened to him. He'd been dumped off his horse on Cheltenham racecourse and the sound in his ears had nothing to do with any cheering. The Festival crowd was a mile off, down the hill.

'Are you all right, lad?'

The voice came from behind him, cutting through the noise in his head, and he lifted his head to see a uniformed figure running towards him.

'I'm fine,' he called, trying to inject certainty into his voice, though it still came out in a croak. His mouth was parched and his head felt as if it had been used for a football. It probably had been. One of the many dangers of being thrown in the middle of a pack of racing horses was the chance of catching a flying hoof on the helmet.

The fall must have knocked him cold, although not for long as the St John's Ambulance man had only just reached him. Charlie managed a grin.

'I just need to catch my breath,' he said. The truth was, he didn't think

78

he could stand yet. He'd be OK in a minute though. He'd been in this situation before.

It was important not to let on how badly he'd been hurt or he wouldn't be allowed to carry on. This was Cheltenham, the top meeting of the season. No self-respecting jockey would let a bit of concussion keep him out of that.

There was another reason too but he couldn't think of it just at the moment.

He made it to the ambulance without wobbling around too much and was thankful for the ride back. A young doctor put him through a battery of tests which, fortunately, Charlie was familiar with. He firmly denied that he'd been knocked out but it was twenty minutes before they let him go.

He found Ben Sayers waiting for him. He looked as relieved as Charlie felt.

'That was close,' Ben said. 'I

thought I was going to have to find another rider.'

The fog in Charlie's head cleared a little. He remembered now that Ben had booked him to ride Smokescreen in the Gold Cup. No wonder the trainer was asking after his health.

As he changed into the colours of Christina Marcus, Charlie reckoned he'd be OK. He had a heck of a headache but at least his legs no longer felt as if they were made out of jelly. They'd have to knock his head off his shoulders for him to miss a ride in the Gold Cup. After all, it was going to be his last.

This was his final season as a jockey. Riding races over jumps was a young man's game and he was thirty-six next birthday. He'd decided months ago to try his hand at training instead. Accidents like the one today just proved what a good decision that was.

Was the ride in his last Gold Cup what he'd been trying to remember?

No. It was something else but he couldn't get at it. It was obviously important but there were more urgent matters to deal with. Like how he was going to steer half a tonne of horse over three and a quarter miles and twenty-two stiff fences and finish ahead of a dozen of the best steeplechasers in the world.

CHAPTER FOURTEEN

If Alan had a complaint about Cheltenham on Gold Cup day it was simply that there were too many damn people. It was impossible to get away from them, especially the Irish, getting drunker and noisier as the day wore on. Frankly, there was only so much booze-fuelled jollity a man could take.

In past years, he'd pushed the boat out. Booked a suite in the best hotel and stayed for the entire Festival.

He'd hired boxes and chalets, entertaining corporate guests to days of lavish hospitality. It was all in the cause of business, naturally, but it would have been wonderful if one of his many horses over the years had won the biggest prize in front of his best customers. But he'd had no luck in the Gold Cup and he'd wearied of the effort of entertaining on a grand scale.

Today he'd flown in by helicopter with Matilda Hurst and they'd lunched briefly but well in one of the on-course restaurants. He had a car laid on for later to whisk the pair of them off to his favourite manor-house hotel in the Cotswolds. God willing, the small golden trophy that he'd coveted so long would make the journey with them.

The centre of the parade ring was almost as crowded as the viewing area outside it. Trainers, owners and their many friends and allies— known in the trade as a horse's 'connections'—huddled together in excited groups. They were bundled up in overcoats and wax jackets against the wet March wind, sporting every dull shade in the spectrum, from navy to brown to beige. Fortunately the jockeys, now stepping into the ring in their bright silks, supplied a note of colour.

So too did a ravishing blonde woman in a fuchsia-pink jacket and a white scarf. Typical bloody Christina, thought Alan, out to draw attention to herself. Everywhere he looked, it seemed, he caught a glimpse of his ex-wife out of the corner of his eye.

'Oh, Alan, just look at him.' Matilda Hurst was at his elbow. On reflection, her glistening copper hair and porcelain skin made her as eye-catching as Christina, if you liked those kind of looks. Increasingly, Alan found that he did.

She was pointing towards Devil Moon as he was led around the ring. As Liam had promised, he looked ready to run for his life.

'He's magnificent,' said Hurst. 'I'm almost inclined to put some money on him.'

'You've left it a bit late,' he growled. The green letters on the giant electronic screen which displayed the betting odds showed Devil Moon as the clear favourite.

'I said almost. I still think Smokescreen's going to win.' She was grinning at him.

He'd have snapped at her, risen to the bait, if a chime hadn't sounded from inside her coat. Her mobile phone. The damned thing had been going off ever since they'd got here.

He'd have told her to switch it off for good if she hadn't stepped away to take the call. And he found himself staring past a knot of people straight at Christina. She looked through him as if he didn't exist.

He turned away. The sooner the race started the better.

CHAPTER FIFTEEN

Charlie Stubbs had known a lot of owners in his time. Some knew everything about horses. Others didn't know which end the food went in or where it came out. A few were mean-spirited, most were generous to a fault and several he'd count as good friends. But none were as pretty as the owner of Smokescreen. She was nice with it, too.

'Are you certain you're well enough to ride?' she asked.

'Sure I am. The doc gave me the OK just now.'

She looked doubtful. 'Just make sure you come back safe. You and the horse—that's the most important thing.'

He nodded. All owners said that before tough steeplechases, but in this case he could tell she meant it. Some of them wouldn't care if you broke your neck provided their beast got over the line first.

Ben gave him a lift-up into Smokescreen's saddle and delivered his last-minute instructions.

Charlie nodded, but little of what he heard seemed to register. Ben's words were all jumbled up in his aching head. Too bad. He wasn't going to back out now.

*   *   *

'What did you just say?' Alan hissed, keeping his voice low with an effort. He didn't want to make a scene in the middle of the parade ring but what Matilda Hurst had just told him filled him with instant fury.

She was tucking her phone back into her coat pocket. 'I said I've got to go. At once.'

'Before the race?' Alan was astounded.

'I'm really sorry. It's bad timing, I know, but I must get back to

London.'

'How on earth do you think you're going to do that?'

'Helicopter. I fixed it earlier when I thought there was a chance I might have to leave in a hurry.'

He couldn't believe what he was hearing. She'd let him squire her around the course, buy her lunch, introduce her to some of the top racing folk in the land and all the time she was planning to leave him in the lurch.

'And what's so all-fired important that you choose this moment to walk out on me?'

She hesitated. 'I shouldn't mention it but I suppose you're going to find out shortly. Thimbles have had another offer. It's more money and there's a guarantee on jobs. No redundancies.'

Her words sucked the fury from his body. He felt numb from the blow.

'What offer?' he said.

'Payne Robinson.' She named the leading supermarket chain in the country. His biggest rivals.

She laid a small hand on his sleeve. 'Sorry, Alan. Good luck with Devil Moon.'

'Hang on, Tilly. What about tonight? I've booked the hotel.'

She looked at him coldly. 'I'm sure you can find another girl to keep you company. We're all pretty much the same to you, aren't we?'

He watched her go through the crowd.

She'd stitched him up. She'd picked his mind and body like a thief. The ruthless little bitch.

So who cared about her green eyes and copper hair and Cotswold hotels and those clapped-out West Country convenience stores? More trouble than they were worth and Payne bloody Robinson were welcome to them. He'd had a lucky escape, it was obvious.

'Do you really think that?' his

father murmured softly in his head. 'Just for once, Alan, have you ever considered that you might be in the wrong?'

Of course he had. He wasn't a child.

Christina was in his eye line again, standing close to Ben. Another woman who'd run away from him.

Suddenly he realised what he should do. It wouldn't mend any of his broken relationships—it probably wouldn't make any difference to the events of the day—but it might just keep his father quiet.

He looked around the parade ring. There was someone he had to talk to urgently. Time to cancel his insurance.

But the horses were leaving and the crowd was beginning to break up.

It was too late.

CHAPTER SIXTEEN

As Charlie cantered down to the start he began to relax. It was a relief to know he didn't have to watch his words any longer. He could talk to the animal beneath him with a nudge of the knee and a tug on the rein. People were a darn sight more complicated.

He jostled with the other runners and riders at the start. Jockeys and horses alike looked nervous. Riders' faces were pale and some horses were sweating up, despite the chilly breeze. Charlie remembered that this was the Gold Cup, a race that made even the coolest hot under the collar. But not him—not today anyway. It was as if he was in a dream.

He almost got caught out when the starting tapes went up and the others leapt forward as if it was a cavalry charge. But Smokescreen was eager not to get left behind and ran after them before Charlie had urged him on.

After that, he got a grip. He'd been a bit worried about the first few fences—the last thing he needed was to be shot out of the saddle again. But Smokie was a sound jumper, smart enough to adjust his stride so he sailed neatly over the obstacles. Charlie began to feel his confidence grow.

*   *   *

Alan watched the race on the screen in the bar. What was the point in standing in the crush in the stands when the action was miles off? Television gave a much better picture. Besides, he needed a drink.

He wasn't thinking about Christina or Matilda Hurst or his father. Or the conversation he wished he'd been able to have before the race. It was too late now for regrets. The horses were running and things were no longer in his control.

Alan felt distanced from events on the screen. Devil Moon was eating up the ground with his enormous stride, sailing over the fences like a bird, waiting for his chance to leave the rest of the field for dead. He'd won the King George VI at Kempton and the Pillar Chase on this same course. He was the short-price favourite for the race and he was perfectly positioned. Maybe this was going to be Alan's year after all.

The funny thing was, he wasn't sure how much he really cared.

*   *   *

'How's he doing?'

Christina was facing away from the course with her head buried in Ben's chest. From the moment Smokescreen had nearly been left behind at the start, she hadn't been able to look.

'Smokie's doing fine,' he said into the thick tangle of her hair. 'Charlie's just easing him into the race. I told you he knew what he was doing.'

Ben was trying hard to keep his emotions under control. This was the toughest part of his job, watching the race. Like all trainers, he was close to the animals he trained, closer than their owners. They were his babies. But he could do nothing for them once the contest started.

He often had two runners in the same race and he could honestly say he never favoured one over the other. He wanted them to do well in the same measure. That was the proper attitude for an experienced trainer like himself.

But it was hard to keep this up with Christina in his arms. She'd swept his old life away like a tidal wave. He was in love. It was only natural that, beneath his professional air, he should want her horse to win.

'What's happening now?' Christina said. She was trembling. He fancied he could feel her heart beating against his.

Out on the course, the race was approaching its climax as a dozen thundering racehorses began their charge down the hill to the winning post.

'Open your eyes, Christina,' he said. 'You've got to watch this.'

*　　　*　　　*

Charlie had ridden in the Gold Cup many times without ever being on the winner. He'd had a decent enough career but he'd never worked for the big owners and trainers. As a result, the horses he'd ridden had always been outsiders, plucky long shots from small yards who were outgunned on the day. And when Ben had booked him to ride Smokescreen, he'd assumed the horse would turn out to be just another also-ran. But he was wrong.

By the time they'd completed the first circuit of the course, it had dawned on even Charlie's fuddled brain that Smokie was no also-ran. Apart from his jumping skill, he was a long-striding type with a high cruising speed. There seemed no reaction to his long lay-off for injury. On the contrary, he was enjoying himself.

Riding along the far side for the second time, over the water jump and the open ditch, Charlie had noticed that some of the horses around them were beginning to tire. But Smokescreen had had no problem in keeping up with the stiff pace set by the front runners. And now, as they began the downhill gallop to the final two fences, he pushed his horse on. If he could get among the leading bunch there was no knowing what might happen on the run-in to home.

Smokie jumped the second-to-last

as if he had springs in his heels, landing in front of the horse racing in third place. Just ahead of them now was Lantern Jack, a muscular grey who had won the Gold Cup by six lengths two years ago. Charlie reckoned he was past his best. The way Smokie was travelling, he was sure they could take him whenever they wanted.

Second in the Gold Cup in his last season—that would be something to be proud of.

They raced side by side around the last bend, into the home straight with Lantern Jack on the inside, next to the running rail. Smokescreen stormed past him.

It dawned on Charlie that maybe he could do better than second. The horse obviously thought so.

The leader was two lengths ahead as they approached the final fence. Charlie recognised the powerful black animal but he couldn't name him. He still wasn't thinking right.

Smokescreen put in an enormous leap at the last and, when he landed, they were racing neck and neck with their rival.

Devil Moon, that was his name.

Cheltenham is a cruel course of ups and downs and it saves its final twist for the end. The last hundred yards is an uphill slog that drains the remaining dregs of strength from empty lungs and tired legs. Only a horse with a big heart wins a sprint finish in front of a baying crowd at Cheltenham. And both Smokescreen and Devil Moon possessed that.

The two horses were flying up the slope in front of fifty thousand screaming people towards a winning post that seemed never to get closer.

Charlie couldn't hear a sound. He was in a bubble, sealed off from everything except his one last chance for the glory. But a picture had emerged from the fog that was clogging up his brain. A man in a suit with eyes like a winter sky—Devil

Moon's owner, Alan Marcus.

To his left, the black horse wobbled and his stride shortened, as if his reserves of strength and energy had finally run out. Then he was gone and Charlie and Smokescreen were in the lead with the post just twenty yards off.

Suddenly the fog in Charlie's head vanished and the nagging thought that had eluded him since his fall became clear.

Alan had promised Charlie half a dozen horses next season to help him set up in business as trainer. All he had to do was make sure that Smokescreen did not win the race.

Well, thought Charlie, as they flashed across the line in first place, there was nothing he could do about it now. What's more, as he stood up in his stirrups to receive the tumultuous applause that was his due, he wouldn't have wished things any different.